Spring Fairies
Seasons Series

Discover the enchanting world of "Spring Fairies" in the hidden realm of "Blossom Glade." The remarkable fairies, led by Aurora, the bringer of warmth, are on a mission to protect the delicate Balance of Spring. As winter's chill recedes, they emerge with glistening wings, ushering in the beauty of spring.

"Spring Fairies" **companion COLORING BOOK** provides an engaging, relaxing, and creative experience for all ages. Join the fairies on through their adventures, one color at a time, and watch as the world around them burst to life in this captivating coloring adventure.

by
Deborah Wolschrijn
https://www.amazon.com/author/weplaywelearn

"Seasons" Series Book Titles

The "Seasons" series contains these magical titles
available in hardcover, paperback or on Kindle
and, of course, beautifully illustrated and in in brilliant color.

Order on
Amazon.com

Spring Fairies

Discover the enchanting world of "Spring Fairies" in the hidden realm of "Blossom Glade." The remarkable fairies, led by Aurora, the bringer of warmth, are on a mission to protect the delicate Balance of Spring.

Summer Fairies

Summer Faires takes place in the mystical realm of Sunflower Glade and Solstice Meadow.
A captivating summer tale unfolds, centered on Twinkle and Leon, whose love defied all odds.

Autmn Fairies

Introducing "Autumn Fairies: A Magical Adventure"! As the Autumn Fairies gracefully guide each leaf to the ground, they weave a vibrant tapestry from the colors of the enchanted woods. Join us on a captivating journey.

Winter Fairies

Prepare to be transported to the enchanting world of 'Winter Haven', a 'Winter Fairy's Tale.' In this captivating story, you'll journey alongside the graceful Winter Fairies as they dance their way through their magical realm.

SPRING FAIRIES, A SEASONS SERIES TITLE

In the hidden corners of Blossom Glade, concealed among blooming fields and the sweet scent of flowers, there thrived a secret realm known as Spring Haven. Within this magical expanse, a remarkable group of beings known as the Spring Fairies made their home, and in the heart of this enchanting world, a captivating tale unfolded.

As winter's icy grip reluctantly loosened, the Spring Fairies emerged from their cozy nooks, their wings glistening like dew-kissed petals. Among them was Aurora, the bringer of warmth, and guardian of the delicate Balance of Spring. With each flutter of her wings, she chased away the remnants of winter's chill, allowing the first whispers of spring to awaken.

Aurora and her fellow fairies knew they must act swiftly to "save the bees." With determination in their hearts, they set out to restore the bee population. They danced among the bee hives, their gentle touch rousing the bees from their slumber. Through a magical connection, they communicated with the bees, promising to protect them and their precious honey.

In their quest to save the bees, the fairies encountered unforeseen challenges—marauding wasps and unpredictable weather—but they persevered with unwavering resolve. Together with their friends, the butterflies and dragonflies, they formed an alliance to safeguard the fragile ecosystem of Blossom Glade.

As the fairies work tirelessly to restore balance and harmony, their invisible presence is felt in the laughter of children playing in meadows, the buzzing of bees, and the graceful dance of butterflies. It is a symphony of life, a testament to the Spring Fairies' unwavering dedication.

Year-after-year, their magic does reside,

Spring Fairies in flight, their wings open wide.

Winter's chill gives way to the changing season's

warm embrace,

The fairies magic continues to awaken the world with

delicate grace.

Aurora, the bringer of light, will always lead the crew so bright,

Chasing away the cold, as their wings take flight.

On a quest as friends to take care of the bees with all their might,

Protecting the balance of nature, making everything right.

The fairies fly in fields of flowers with butterflies

and dragonflies, they did play,

Hidden from human eyes, in the light of day.

But their work was a marvel, a true delight to see,

In the heart of Spring Haven, where all things Spring

came to be.

As daffodils and tulips awakened from their rest,

The Spring Fairies' magic is at its very best.

Invisible, yet present, they filled the world with glee,

In Blossom Glade, where spring's dreams set hearts free.

Printed in Great Britain
by Amazon

37419963R00016

But this year, a grave challenge befell Spring Haven—a looming threat to the delicate Balance of Spring. The once-drowsy bees were in peril. Their numbers dwindled, and without their vital role in pollination, the future of Spring Haven and the surrounding world hung in the balance.